For my dozen splendid cousins ~ MH

In memory of Paul and Tommy,
Who Championed Life ~ SZ

First published in Australia in 2025
by Thames & Hudson Australia
Wurundjeri Country, 132A Gwynne Street
Cremorne, Victoria 3121

First published in the United States of America in 2026
by Thames & Hudson Inc.
500 Fifth Avenue
New York, New York 10110

28 27 26   5 4 3 2

ISBN 978-1-760-76488-3
ISBN 978-1-760-76524-8 (U.S. edition)

NATIONAL LIBRARY OF AUSTRALIA
A catalogue record for this book is available from the National Library of Australia

Library of Congress Control Number 2025935958

Design: Sasha Beekman
Printed and bound in China by C&C Offset Printing Co., Ltd

FSC www.fsc.org MIX Paper | Supporting responsible forestry FSC® C008047

Thames & Hudson Australia wishes to acknowledge that Aboriginal and Torres Strait Islander peoples are the first storytellers of this nation and the Traditional Custodians of the land on which we live and work. We acknowledge their continuing culture and pay respect to Elders past and present.

HERE COME THE COUSINS

Maggie Hutchings & Sarah Zweck

I count down the days all year until ...

Seven smiling cousins
burst through Pop's door.

We swing each other round
so fast we get dizzy!

Then it's rock paper scissors for the high bunks!

We can't wait to wriggle into our swimmers
but before we do ...

We stop by the door post to measure who
grew most since last summer.

It's *never* me.

Our days are sandy and sunny.

Cousins speckled with sea salt!
Cousins striped with zebra zinc!
Cousins duck-diving deeper than we should!

Aunty Moira shouts, ‘Stay close to shore!’

Mum hollers, 'Don't forget the sunscreen!'

Uncle Ezra calls out,
'Don't splash the small ones!'

While the grown-ups aren't watching
we clamber up Whale Rock and

JUMP!

When Pop rings the lunchtime bell
we race, salty hair flying, feet burning, yelling,
'Last one there gets the wobbly chair!'

Our afternoons are shady and snoozy.

Cousins curled like kittens in Pop's hammock.
Cousins deep in dusty books from Pop's shelves.
Cousins swapping secrets in Pop's tree fort.

Until the sea calls us
for one last lazy sunset swim.

Our nights are stories and starlight.

We play snakes and ladders
while the grown-ups tell tales
of other summers.

We've heard them *all* before
but we don't mind.

We swarm around Pop
singing, 'We want to see the pictures!'

Then like a magic door the old album opens.

Aunty Moira snorkelling *far* from shore!

Mum sunburnt *and* peeling!

Uncle Ezra splashing *everyone*!

And Pop backflipping off the top of Whale Rock!

When summer ends
seven cousins say goodbye.

One of us always cries.

It’s usually me.

But when seven voices shout,
'See you next summer!'

I can’t help smiling.
I shout out, ‘I’m going to be the tallest next year!’
And …

... I start counting down the days.